For my father, Joseph R. Grant
- Nahjee

For more information please visit:
www.nahjeegrant.com

ALL CHILDREN EQUAL SUCCESS

The WORLD was made for YOU!

Written By Nahjee Grant

Illustrated By Justine Babcock

Hello, my little Bamboo Shoot.

I'm so glad you're in this world!

To me, your smile is

brighter than the sun.

You are a treasure!

Shiny and new!

You are my hero and

nothing inspires me more

than seeing you succeed.

Wish big and dream bigger.

Find something you love and

give it everything you have.

You have a heart full of gold.

Polish it so the world

can see it shine.

Lead by example and motivate others. When you soar together, you can soar higher!

Don't be afraid to face your

fears and try something new.

Your faith will carry you through!

Embrace the ever-changing seasons of life and grow into the best this world has to offer.

The world is wide open

for you to explore!

Throughout your life you

will be tested, but you are strong.

Always keep your head to the

sky and take a leap!

Starlight travels millions of miles

to bless you with its glow.

Get a great view so you

know how big the world is

and your place in it.

Put love into the world and it will come

back. What happens next is up to you.

You are a blessing in so many ways.

I have faith in you.